The Airborne Ghost

An aviation tale of our times

Martin Leusby

About the Author

Martin Leusby is a private pilot with over 3000 hours flying experience, based in South-East England.

He has competed in sporting aviation and represented his country, and now flies on behalf of the emergency services – which is quite unusual on a private licence.

Martin has written articles for aviation magazines including such as Pilot Magazine, Flyer, and AOPA. During the recent pandemic lockdown, he wrote this book – his first novella. It was received so well that he has now written a memoir of his almost 40 years of flying "Pilots Progress".

About this Book

The aviation thriller "The Airborne Ghost" is 20,000 words – a novella which is 85% true and tells the story of a British private pilot visiting Paris - where he sees something that results in an airborne pursuit across Europe and puts him in a life-threatening situation.

Written for other pilots, who will understand the technicalities of both the detective work and the journey, it will be appreciated by anyone with an aviation interest who enjoys a real page-turner!

The question is……....will he get back safely?

Reviews

It's clear that Martin has used his aviation experience to good effect, as the book has more relevant aviation detail than pretty much any other novel or short story I can think of **- Ian Seager, Editor, Flyer Magazine.**

A crime drama focused on the General Aviation scene in the UK and Europe. The Airborne Ghost is entertainingly written in a very enjoyable style. Setting the story in the immediate post-Covid era makes it both contemporary and relevant. I really enjoyed this book – easy to read and amusing in places **- Steve Bridgewater, Editor, AOPA Magazine.**

Introduction

This story began as a planning exercise, to while away some time in lockdown, and once I researched destinations, it became a series of reminisces as well as a tale. Many pilots and others will recognise some of the characters within this story, who are real people, as are many of the events described, and the places - which are all real. If you are mentioned then it is done so in friendship and respect, and I trust you will forgive me for using your real names.

Traditionally authors thank people who made it possible. In my case I would like to thank not only everyone who has ever made my flying possible, but particularly the NHS without whose skills I might not have lived, never mind fly – and particularly Mr "Dickie" Barrington, the Kettering-based orthopaedic surgeon who bolted me back together, and all today's heroes who are ensuring we get through the pandemic.

I realise the tale probably has a "sell-by date" as we near the end to lockdown and move towards our semi-dystopian future, and trust that some of the difficulties foretold will not actually occur, or that at least we will recover from them in the short-term.

For non-aviators who read this (there may be a few?) I have included a glossary of most of the terms you may not recognise, after the end of the story.

To Colin. Looking forward to flying with you again.

Morning had broken

In more ways than one. Since the pandemic, and several months after the vaccine was found, nearly all of Europe was open again, desperate to get their economies moving. About 93% of the population had been vaccinated and the authorities deemed that was enough to allow travel again. There would always be some conspiracy theorists that refused vaccination, but everyone had had the opportunity, and if they wished to risk their lives still, their effect on national health services would be minimal.

Now, the early fog at Rochester Airport was beginning to lift. Being 426 feet above sea level, it was always later than in surrounding areas, but on occasions the airfield could have good visibility and blue skies whilst the valleys below were filled with mist or worse.

The forecast was for improving conditions with gentle winds – all boding well for today's new adventure. The shorter autumn days meant there was no time to be lost, so the pilot started his pre-flight check of his rather old Cessna. Old it might be, but the new, more powerful engine had made a vast difference to its performance, and the extra speed would make for a faster transit to their destination.

Rochester still lacked the hard runway it desperately needed, so after the recent heavy, prolonged rains, he knew he would need to use soft field take-off procedures to unstick from Runway 20. Whilst moving around the aircraft checking everything was in order, he could feel the softness of the grass parking area and realised even taxying would need to be slow with gentle turns so as not to cut up the surfaces.

It would be good to finally fly with company aboard. Ever since the first lockdown, he had kept to solo flight only, as social distancing was impossible in a small craft, and he valued his life and licence too much to risk death, or possibly worse, long-COVID and loss of his medical.

He had just finished the external checks when Colin (whom he laughingly called his victim) arrived. They had flown together a lot pre-COVID and normally Colin was always waiting for him to arrive at the airfield when he knew there was a trip to be had, but today he was relatively late, and promised to explain later. Many years previously, Colin had wanted to be a pilot himself, but health reasons tripped him up, and despite having had several lessons, had had to decide to become an inveterate passenger. He would fly with anybody, in anything, to anywhere – he just needed to get into the air to be happy, and soon amassed many more hours aloft than most private pilots ever achieve.

Both strapped in and it was time to fire up the Lycoming engine, and check systems. Oil pressure was immediate, but temperature took its time as expected. Whilst waiting for warmth, electrics were switched on – radios first, and then the various electronic devices he had added to the analogue-instrumented aircraft. Wealthier owners have spent fortunes on updating panels with the latest digital instruments, but this Luddite had only added portable devices he knew would be cheaper to update as technology advanced.

Despite that, the essential kit was in. There had been no choice as to whether to install the new 8.33 MHz spaced radio, but the old King 155 radio with VOR and ILS was retained as a get out of trouble if weather made a cloud-break difficult. Although ILS systems were being withdrawn across Europe, the replacement RNAV approaches were not common enough yet, so for now, the Instrument Landing System remained.

Whilst taught to use a checklist to run through procedures,

the pilot was so familiar with the aircraft he had owned for more than 30 years, that he did it by rote instead. Naughty really, but it worked for him, and the checklist was in the pocket by his left foot in case something occurred that meant he needed to refer to it.

If anything were to be forgotten, he would admit it would be to push the ALT button on the transponder. This would alert any radar watchers of his height – but as controllers could see his registration on their screens, displayed by the Mode S transponder, they would remind him with "no Mode Charlie observed", and he would push the appropriate button whilst apologising.

Conspicuity was the buzzword of the moment, and he turned on the SkyEcho2 to start acquiring its GPS signal. The CAA had only recently started allowing the ADS-B Out facility at same time as his Mode S transponder – but were now actively encouraging the same, even offering rebates to purchasers of new equipment. For once, he had bought too soon, as the deal was not retrospective!

The SkyEcho was attached to the right side of the windscreen and was connected by Wi-Fi to his phone, which was mounted on the side of the windscreen to his left. The phone was programmed with SkyDemon so that he not only had navigation data, but warnings of other aircraft transmitting ADS-B Out and even gliders that gave off FLARM signals. The icing on the cake was his Bluetooth headset which meant he received verbal warnings of airfields and airspace ahead, and should traffic be getting too close, the nice lady's voice would tell him with details of just how close.

She also said where to look and whether their course was reciprocal, converging or whatever. That way he did not need to constantly look at the phone, but could keep his gaze outside the aircraft, scanning as he was trained. And he had bought the expensive headsets when converting to the new 8.33 radio, and been able to take advantage of the rebate scheme the CAA had introduced for that – what was not to like?

Despite being happy with this set-up, when planning he still programmed his routes into the Garmin 496 portable GPS that attached to the yoke and drew lines on charts in case any jamming trials or other situations wiped out his GPS signals.

Colin had stowed his holdall on the rear seats, before donning his lifejacket, but made sure he had kept his notebook and camera handy for any eventuality. Having flown together so often, normally the pilot did not feel the need to brief Colin before the flight, but as today was both over water and overseas, ran through necessary actions they would take if circumstances insisted. A final check that they both remembered their passports and they were ready to commit aviation!

The Prospect of Le Bourget

Flight plans had been filed the previous day, as had a General Aviation Report submitted to inform HM Border Force and Customs of who they were and where they were going to and coming from. As they taxied gently towards the holding point for Runway 20, Colin was excited. Although he had flown in and out of many an airstrip with the pilot, they had mainly been in England and the prospect of a new airfield in France going into his logbook, and a visit to the Musée de l'Air et de l'Espace at Le Bourget was something special.

The pilot had considered flying direct into Le Bourget, but the main Paris Airports are pretty unfriendly to General Aviation (only Le Bourget allowing non-commercial flights), and the prospective costs of landing, handling, parking and security fees would have approached 1000 Euros – all for an aircraft weighing less than one tonne. Furthermore, all approaches and departures would have had to be under Instrument Flight Rules and he would have to purchase and carry a great deal of documentation.

Add to that, the Avgas he would need to return was not available at Le Bourget (LFPB), and so he had filed for Lognes Émerainville (LFPL). Just to the east of central Paris, they had an excellent reputation for friendliness and inexpensive fees for private pilots, and staff had even been known to give lifts to the local RER station. A 5 Euro fare would get them to the centre, and then on to the museum.

Power and control checks complete, they lined up and departed 20. Initial routing was virtually due south to Hastings, where they would coast out and turn for Abbeville. This would avoid the NOTAM'd pollution patrols that were operating that day and being as high as they could for the crossing, they would be well above the drones being used to patrol the Channel for illegal immigrants in boats.

Once past Maidstone, the London Terminal Area base was raised to 3500 feet, so they could climb through the remnants of the morning fog into the bright sunshine above. From Abbeville they would route to the town of Meaux, not quite in a straight line as in the last few miles of that leg, they would skirt around Paris CTR, and drop below 1500 feet to remain below the TMA.

Once overhead Meaux, another turn and 13 nautical miles would bring them to Lognes, where the choice would be 700 metres of asphalt runway or 1000 metres of grass. Whilst the asphalt was only 20m wide versus 100m wide grass, taxying would be shorter, and the pilot was happy with that.

Having changed frequency from Rochester to Lydd for the crossing, they were informed that the HMCG chopper was on station off Dungeness. No doubt they had found another RIB full of migrants. The leg from Hastings to Abbeville meant 50 nautical miles and half an hour over water, so once past Headcorn they began the climb to 5300 feet, which they maintained until the LTMA was replaced by the Worthing CTA and they could climb even higher to take advantage of the prevailing westerly winds. The pilot was following the Take Two rule and this time, had remembered to push the ALT button.

Colin listened carefully to the beat of the O-360 Lycoming. He did not know why but he always sensed engines sounded different over water. The pilot told him the maximum they could fly at would be FL75 (73 with Take Two) and that would give them a maximum glide range of about 13 nautical miles, or a little more taking account of the tailwind.

That was just as long as he reacted quickly enough when it all went quiet. Having said that, he was confident in the recently installed engine, and the SkyDemon helpfully showed his gliding range around the image of his aircraft, which was comforting as they neared the coast just south of Berck-sur-Mer.

Vive la France

Having informed Paris North Information of his Frontier Crossing, he transferred to Abbeville, whom he would overfly in the turn to Meaux. They did not want to know and suggested return to Paris Information. He had tried.

Shortly after turning, Amiens slipped by to port and made a good reference point to check his calculated ground speed, in an otherwise featureless area of country. Whilst all the modern kit gave him estimates of his next turning point, old habits die hard, and it was good to practice. In fact, the higher winds were really helping, and it looked as if the whole flight would take less than 2 hours. Which would be helpful if they needed to walk the 25 minutes to the RER station.

Once past Montdidier and the large mast just southwest, it was necessary to descend below the restricted area R205/5 and then continue to under 1500 feet for the R205/2 and TMA Paris-2 – which necessitated a call to Meaux on 120.150 as they would be low and skirting around them. The pilot had hoped they would speak English and was relieved when they did.

It was good to see that Meaux had an 8.33 MHz-spaced frequency, as EASA had insisted was necessary for everyone. The only exceptions he knew about were emergency frequencies, such as Distress and Diversion on 121.5 - which he could tune into on the older King 155 if the newer radio failed.

Soon Lognes appeared, just inside the outer edge of Paris, and by paralleling the autoroute, the pilot set up for a straight-in approach to 26 Right, the narrower, but hard runway. Despite the relatively short flight, he was looking forward to stretching his legs and making use of other facilities.

Before calling Lognes Radio on 118.600 with his registration, the pilot had checked his crib sheet, and was ready to state "a destination de vos installation", but was surprised when the controller replied with "we have your details and position – grass is unavailable, make a straight-in to 26 hard, call at Echo". Echo was the VRP road junction in line with the runway, and just North of the nearby Chateau de Ferrières. By then they would be inside the RMZ. This was too easy and gave him no opportunity to impress Colin!

In due course they touched down and turned gently off onto November taxiway to reach the parking area in front of the tower. "Park at Alpha 2 alongside other Cessna Sierra Mike" came the instruction. The pilot duly complied and found himself alongside another British aircraft G-CFSM. He busied himself with recording time for the log and then powering down his electronics before checking magnetos and shutting down the engine.

He had not noticed Colin staring at the aircraft alongside and looking extremely puzzled. "Something's wrong here" said Colin. "That aircraft doesn't exist…………"

Airborne Encyclopaedia

Colin was a walking reference book when it came to aviation and airframes. Over the years he had amassed an enormous private collection of photographs and recorded many a registration on his travels. He did not admit to being an aircraft-spotter as such, but he surely was, yet with a much greater depth of information about aviation. His interests even stretched to buses and trains, but not to the same level – anything to do with transport was important, but not as high in his interest as aviation.

The pilot respected his opinion. "What do you mean?".

"G-CFSM used to be a banner-towing aircraft. It was blown over at Manston about six years ago and written off – completely destroyed". The pilot remembered. It used to be Simon's aircraft. Simon, who was tragically killed with David, another of his friends, as they were ferrying an aircraft back from Portugal. Two very experienced pilots, yet they had managed to fly into a Spanish mountain.

From the cockpit, he looked at the other aircraft. It was similar to that of Simon, mainly white with blue and yellow accents, but instead of the banner-towing company logo on the tail, it had a roundel with Médecins sans Frontières emblazoned on it. It also did not *look* like a Cessna 172Q Cutlass, but something very similar. He knew all about the Cutlass, because by upgrading his own aircraft to 180HP, effectively he had created a 172Q from a 172H. There was only one Cutlass remaining in the UK after Simon's blew over, and that had been recently sold to Northern Ireland.

Colin thought it could be a 172 Rheims Rocket – which has an even bigger engine, and the beefier tail was the clue, along with the fact it had a three-blade propellor fitted. But why would anyone want to clone a "dead" registration?

The CAA does not allow any registration to be used again.

The pilot was certain of this because he had once registered a homebuilt kit he was building with a partner, with his initials, and when the build time seemed interminable, he finally gave up and bought a ready-made aeroplane, and then found he was unable to transfer the registration.

Something was rotten in Denmark, as they say. Just then, the occupants of the other Cessna began to disembark and unload their cargo. From the luggage bay each of them took out what looked like a cool box – the type of thing you'd take on a picnic – but as they were close by, the pilot could read the legend "Blood and Transplant" below the NHS logo on the side of the boxes. Fastened with tie-wraps, one box had a large red label stating "Right Kidney", and the other a similarly large label (yellow this time) stating "Left Kidney". Dressed in jeans and wearing tee-shirts with the MSF logo, the two strode towards the large letter C displayed on the control tower and were soon gone from sight.

Le Dilemme

It had all looked sensible. A mercy flight delivering much-needed transplant organs, obviously from the UK. But the pilot had a suspicious mind. He had recently become one of the very first Community Policing Volunteers (Aviation) in the country. This after working as a volunteer for Air Search for several years, helping the Kent Resilience Forum and accepting tasks as required by any of the Emergency Services - whether assisting with pollution exercises or photographing fires and floods – or even tower blocks and their escape routes following Grenfell. Whenever there was a need for eyes in the sky, he was there (weather permitting), and it meant he could use his skills to pay back into the system that had saved his life after a serious car accident in 1985.

The CPV (Aviation) role was created by Kent Police, who even before the pandemic, thought of the prospective disruption that would be caused by Brexit, and realised a view of traffic from the air (at no cost to the taxpayer) could be useful. The process of vetting candidates, and interviews continued despite COVID, albeit social distancing needs meant a combination of emails and MS Teams interviews.

Fortunately, all the Air Search team were known to their volunteer liaison officers, so identities could be verified easily. Before the vaccine became available, the urgency increased as they could be useful viewing illegal gatherings, or even the expected civil disturbances.

Back to the current quandary. On the face of it, two well-meaning individuals were probably about to save one or even two lives – but why on earth would they do so in an aircraft with a fictitious registration?

His mind went back to the nineties when he had been instrumental in foiling airborne smugglers in the Midlands.

He had thought it must be drugs, yet it ended up as only rolling tobacco, but it cost the smugglers heavy fines, and impounding of their aircraft and car. It cost the pilot too, as some time later, his own car, left for the weekend at his home base where the incident had occurred, was utterly vandalised with every window smashed and every panel dented. Nothing to link to the smugglers, of course……….

Could this be something similar? If you wanted to bring something into a country without it being examined, what better way than in a medical box, sealed shut and not to be opened until at the receiving hospital? The logo on the aircraft and shirts would lend credence to the story, and it would be an unusual customs officer that would delay the cargo on its mission.

He shared his suspicions with Colin, and they determined they would try to find out more before deciding the next move.

Bienvenue à Lognes

Having called for the bowser to refuel them, by the time they reached the reception desk, the invoice was ready, and he grimaced slightly whilst using the credit card reader. Whilst UK was never going to be as cheap as USA to fly, at least it was not as expensive as France when it came to Avgas! Pretty soon, Avgas low-lead was due to be banned in Europe, and no doubt that would mean another price-hike for the alternative UL91 – the fuel that was actually cheaper when it was introduced, but now was at least as expensive. But the landing fee at under 20 Euro was a delight for such a busy GA facility, and the friendly receptionist smiled at every transaction.

"Where did our fellow Englishmen come in from in the other Cessna?" tried the pilot. "If you mean Doctor Zahn, he's always in and out here, arriving from Germany – I think he is based there".

"That's odd, zahn is German for tooth – are you sure he's not a dentist?". It must have lost something in the translation, as there was not a flicker of a smile. There was nothing more to be gleaned without voicing their suspicions, and being uncertain of the reaction, they decided to sit in the flight-briefing office where they could use the wi-fi to research some more.

First thing was to try FlightRadar24. Using the search facility, and inputting the registration G-CFSM, brought up a history of flights over the last seven days, of which there were two. The flight had arrived from Bitburg, Germany. But the previous day had started from somewhere close to Berlin. Even the free version of FR24 is a great facility, but it has its limitations as it is dependent on ground stations, and if you are low it may not see you. The nearest field to where Sierra Mike first appeared was Schönhagen - just west and slightly south of Berlin, but that might be just when it was high enough to be seen..........

Next thing to do was to go to the CAA website and G-INFO database. This holds the registration and ownership details of all UK registered aircraft, and includes everything from engine and propellor details, to ARC renewal dates and even whether insurance has been checked. It will even identify de-registered aircraft, and that is where they found G-CFSM. Colin was right. The record showed it was de-registered in March 2016, with the reason given as "permanently withdrawn from use".

A further search for "G-CFSM Manston accident" brought up details of how it was blown onto its back on Christmas Eve, 2013, to be de-registered much later, and the accompanying picture showed it could never be economically repaired.

But how could FlightRadar have recorded the registration of a ghost, as it relies on the Mode S transponder to transmit registration? The pilot pondered. Surely someone couldn't have gone to the trouble of purchasing the scrap and radio kit to steal the identity, and why would they want a "ghost" if they had a perfectly good Cessna they could legally fly between countries? If they had bought the scrap or just the transponder, it was probably from Paul in Caterham, where his farm stores more aircraft (after their demise) than British Airways owns. He knows the value of the spares he sells, and it would not have been cheap.

Of course! Back to G-INFO, and there it was. In the Aircraft Details section it shows the "ICAO 24 bit Aircraft Address", and lists Binary, Hex, and Octal – all the information necessary to clone a transponder to become another aircraft – one that would never conflict as it would never fly again.

It was then that they spotted the tray containing used flight plans that had been faxed up to the tower for onward transmission. Right on top was the flight plan for the Cutlass. At 0900 Zulu tomorrow, Sierra Mike was due to depart for the return trip to Bitburg, and then who knows where.

Despite their early start from Rochester, they had already lost an hour time difference, and with refuelling, passports and customs, and subsequent time spent researching in the FBO, it was now mid-afternoon. "We need to think about the museum, Colin. It's getting late, and we might need to do something different".

Pursuit

They decamped from the FBO and took a cab to the Ibis Marne La Vallée Émerainville, the hotel they had pre-booked for overnight. It was just south of the ring-road overlooking the airport, and from their rooms on the upper floor, they could just see the apron, and aircraft parked there. There was a constant flow of GA aircraft arriving and departing and it seemed everyone else knew this was the place to arrive in Paris.

Colin and the pilot talked through what had happened and what they knew. There were other oddities apart from the fictitious registration. British aircraft, but based in Germany? Médicins Sans Frontières on aircraft and tee-shirts, but NHS logos on the organ transplant boxes? Supposedly an English doctor but with an obviously German name?

More importantly, what to do about it? If the boxes had contained contraband, they would be long gone. The Cessna would leave in the morning, and even if they raised the matter with the authorities now, the French would want to check with the CAA for information. The Cessna would be in Germany by then.

"We should see where it goes. We know it's going to Bitburg, so why not get there ahead of it, and then see what happens, and where it goes from there?"

Using the hotel wi-fi they downloaded the Germany chart onto SkyDemon. Not having planned to visit the Fatherland, they had no paper charts, so were reliant on that and the Garmin (which had the full European database). Whilst supposed to carry current charts, if available and "guaranteed" electronic would suffice – and actually be more up to date than any printed version. With a fallback of a spare device, the pilot was happy. He was even happier that as they had come out of lockdown, he had purchased the latest monthly update from Garmin, so airspace was valid for the next fortnight. Normally he would only update as and when there were major changes that would affect him, such as the establishment of Southend CTR, or the latest Farnborough airspace grab.

Next, they plotted the route from Lognes to Bitburg (EDRB). Even routing via the VORs at Châtillon and Diekirch (as a back-up to GPS) only added a mile or two. They would be en route for about 90 minutes, passing close to the birthplace of his Cessna at Rheims, and briefly passing through Luxembourg.

The border crossings necessitated a flight plan, so SkyDemon again obliged. Whenever subscriptions were renewed, SkyDemon threw in a credit for submitting a few free flight plans, and with COVID rampant, there had been no opportunity to use any except to reach Lognes. Departure time was planned for 0830 Zulu - so they would arrive at Bitburg before Sierra Mike – and duly filed.

Without a printer handy, the PLOG was saved to his pad as well as the phone, but the main points and frequencies were committed to paper too. Whilst the recently fitted GTR225 radio had a database of airfield frequencies, he had not connected it to a GPS yet, so could not use the "nearest station" look-up, and he would rather be prepared.

The Garmin took just seconds to programme – start and finish and two VORs en route, and then it was time to recharge all the kit – SkyEcho 2, Phone, Garmin and for good measure, change batteries in the headset. So much easier to do all this programming on portable devices, rather than in the cockpit, but it meant his flight bag was quite heavy!

Time for dinner and an early night, but it was hard to sleep…………

Second Morning

The breakfast was continental, of course. Being pre-paid, check-out was quick and easy, and they were soon back at the aircraft and setting up electronics. Just in case their prey arrived early, they asked for start before the allotted time and it was allowed. A wise move, as just as they taxied out, they glimpsed Zahn and his colleague coming out from the terminal. With luck they would have changed from Lognes before they came on frequency, and they would be unaware of another aircraft on the same route.

Even before they passed Rheims, the pilot was thinking about Bitburg. Whilst Colin had never been there, he had. In May 2011, he had taken part in a trial there, doing a navigation course in the local area, overflying features such as the Nürburgring racetrack. It was a simple exercise, and the results were all based on elapsed timing, and with his previous experience in the British Precision Pilots Association, it was actually a piece of cake. There were only a few entrants, most in aircraft quite unsuitable for the task – even a twin took part – but the pilots and crews were "trying out" to take part in the RB12 Round Britain Rally.

RB12 was supposed to have been a circumnavigation of the UK, by aircraft, power boats and supercars, with each of the disciplines meeting up every evening in a luxury hotel for dinner, drinks, and sleep. It had sounded a good idea, but whilst the supercars could drive to the hotels, and some hotels may have been adjacent to expensive marinas, it was pretty certain that aircrews would have to be brought by bus from outlying airfields. If you drive a Ferrari or similar, or sail a Sunseeker Predator, then the cost of the fuel and hotel are probably insignificant to you, but the average private pilot will scrape to afford his flying, never mind the upper- class accommodation.

The organisers had set up the trial to encourage (not insignificant) deposits to be placed to join the rally. Indeed, a couple of the participant pilots were enthusiastic enough to do so, but our Cessna-driver was happy enough to win the £100 Pooleys voucher and promise to think about it. Unsurprisingly, despite publicity in aviation magazines, there was never enough enthusiasm and the event folded. It is to be hoped that the others regained their deposits.

Even the BPPA have trouble finding people to compete, and the pilot had managed to fly for the Great Britain Team in world events, in England, France, South Africa and more recently, Portugal. Not that he was world-class, more that he was available, willing to have a go, and had an FAI Sporting Licence (and just enough cash!).

On his last visit to Bitburg, there had been great hopes for the airport. Between 1952 and 1994 it had been a front-line NATO airbase, until at the end of the Cold War it was handed back to the German Government. In 1997 it was briefly home to F-15s and F-16s whilst Spangdahlem was having runway repairs but was then scheduled to become a commercial airport. The nearby Hahn airbase was also being developed – later to be renamed Frankfurt-Hahn at Ryanair's request despite the enormous distance from Frankfurt – and was winning in the race, so when the Luxembourg investor could not raise the necessary guarantees for Bitburg, his operation went bust in October 2012.

Colin and the pilot had flown along in ideal conditions. Cloud was a thin overcast but high, and an increasing southerly wind had saved them a few minutes. They set up to join downwind for 23. The massive concrete runway of 8221 x 148 feet that the Americans had built was still there, but the airport notes said that the taxiway at end of 23 was now disused and if they landed long, they would have to back-track to the taxiway opposite the old tower.

The radio was manned, but from a van that was constantly moving around the airport, as the driver was all things to visitors – marshaller, fueller, receptionist. No customs were available but as an internal EU flight none were required.

It was probably the ideal airport for the ghost to use. Very few people, and no officials, and if leaving for another destination in Germany, no flight plan required. They were free to go where they wanted, with no real trace left.

Early Arrival

Having quickly parked, allowed the bowser to refuel, and settled fuel and the 11 Euro landing fee with the van-driver, they listened out on the Yaesu hand-held for the others to arrive. Despite them leaving Lognes early, and well ahead of the other Cessna's planned departure, they were surprised how soon the following aircraft arrived. Either they had left early too, or their quarry had really pushed it along. If it were a Rheims Rocket with the 210HP engine, they could probably cruise at 125 knots, albeit with extra fuel consumption.

That was worth thinking about. If they were going to follow, they would need to be able to keep up. The combination of O-360-A4M and Sensenich prop meant they had a usual economy cruise of 110 knots, but in the flight test after installation, with full power and at 6000 feet, she had achieved 130 knots, just as promised by Air Plains the kit producer – and never even approached the red line on the rev counter. It was doable.

Not knowing where they were going to be going, they hoped it would not be far, as fuel might be an issue at full power. But the FlightRadar history had suggested somewhere near Berlin (if they were returning) and much further than that and it would be Poland.

With 141 litres on board (5 litres unusable), they had more than 3 hours to bingo fuel at normal cruise, and Poland was just that far. If they did have to firewall the throttle, hopefully the extra fuel burn would be set off against the extra speed to reach the destination. Wherever that was………

It made sense to pick an airfield somewhere around Berlin to book out to with the van-driver, so that if the other Cessna occupants were aware of them, they might not suspect anything. Eggersdorf (EDCE) was the choice – almost at the end of the Bremen FIR and just next to Poland, it was in line with where Sierra Mike had first appeared on FlightRadar, but further away from Bitburg. With it programmed into SkyDemon and Garmin, they would be flying on current maps.

The other Cessna was at the opposite end of the apron. They too refuelled quickly, and as soon as the bowser left, and the van-driver had departed to commence a runway inspection, a black Mercedes E-Class drew up alongside. The driver, in a dark suit, moved quickly to the rear of the car and extracted two roller suitcases from the boot. They were the size for carry-on airline luggage and were in the luggage bay of the Cessna before the Mercedes sped off again.

"Colin – how many Euros do you think you could get in one of those cases?". It was a rhetorical question.

With such a laid-back airport, there was no requirement to call for start, so the other Cessna fired up and asked for taxi, for departure to Schönhagen – which is where it had appeared to come from. Perfect, EDAZ was right underneath their planned track to Eggersdorf and they could land there if that were what they decided to do.

The van-driver was still on the runway but was clearing onto a taxiway and announced "all at your discretion" before returning to the apron. The pilot waited for the other Cessna to reach the midpoint taxiway and begin backtracking before starting his own engine. Doing his power and control checks where he was, he would be ready to go as soon as the other one lifted off, and with such a large runway, no backtrack was actually necessary – as a rule with two up and full fuel, only 130m was needed. Another advantage of the 172H was its relative lightness and with the O-360 and 40 degree flaps it could get in and out of anywhere.

Rapid Departure

Even as it was rolling down the runway, the other Cessna was visible on SkyDemon. As he taxied forward, the nice lady warned him of "traffic – same height crossing right to left".

The plan was to stay far enough behind so as not to seen, but close enough that they could see the other aircraft on SkyDemon. The phone would also display the height difference of traffic as a plus or minus figure, so they could fly higher and look down on Sierra Mike, and the lower Cessna's high wing would prevent any sighting of them.

When they had peered briefly through the windows of the other aircraft at Lognes, there was no sign of TCAS or PAW or SkyEcho on board, so hopefully they would be invisible to them. In fact, there had been little kit in the ghost ship, except a Garmin 430 and GTX335 transponder (ADS-B Out) which meant that it would register via their SkyEcho. On reflection, they had not seen the registration on the panel, either. Sierra Mike was as unremarkable as any Cessna, which no doubt served their purposes.

Airborne just five minutes later, they followed the ghost to altitude. Having departed Runway 23 it meant a right turn and climb to avoid Spandahlem & Büchel military zones, which were from surface to 3700 and 4100 feet respectively.

The other Cessna had already changed to Langen Information on 119.150 and they did the same, but did not transmit, only listened. Unsurprisingly, Sierra Mike was no doubt doing the same and was not heard.

The climb continued and soon they were over Koblenz. The direct track would take them through a corner of the Fritzlar Zone which towered up to Flight Level 100, but above that was Class C airspace and they would need to talk to someone, so hopefully the other Cessna and they would curve around it. Both aircraft continued to climb, and soon the other aircraft levelled at FL90 following the semi-circular rule. The following aircraft continued climbing, until the SkyDemon showed the difference as -0.3.

That height would have taken a long time to reach with the old O-300D engine, but the maximum altitude with the Lycoming was now 17,000 feet, and climbs were quick.

Zahn must have been thinking the same about Frizlar and Class C above, and he turned slightly to avoid the corner of airspace and was high enough to overfly the restricted area just to the east.

By the time they had passed Frizlar, they had been in the air for more than an hour and their airspeed was trueing out at 120 knots. Combined with the earlier flight, that meant the three-hour mark was not far away. The pilot was becoming uncomfortable. He knew that anything approaching four hours, his ankle would start to hurt.

Most of the screws and bolts used to put him together after his accident had been removed, but the two in his right ankle remained and whilst the Cessna only really needed rudder on take-off and landing, the position of his foot on the pedals was guaranteed to cause him to stiffen. The plate that remained in his left wrist and the bolts in his right shoulder were not a problem, except when he rode shotgun in his buddy Rob's Piper Arrow, when he couldn't reach over his shoulder and backwards for the shoulder strap. Much as a break to stretch his legs would be desirable, it was not an option, the Polish border being still nearly two hours away, and the aircraft droned on.

The route was remarkably free of difficult airspace. COVID had decimated the commercial airlines and with it, some airports also failed to survive. Like many other private pilots, when the airlines were first grounded, he had been allowed to shoot approaches at Gatwick, and was even allowed down to 400 feet – something never possible when the airports were active. But Gatwick was now recovering since British Airways had commenced flights from there again. Not so, the upcoming Berlin Brandenberg Airport. When Willy Brandt airport was being built, it was intended to replace Schönefeld as well as Tegel and Tempelhof (which had closed in 2008).

It should have opened in 2011, but suffered massive delays due to poor planning, management, insolvencies of contractors and even corruption. It only received its operating licence in May 2020, with test runs of passenger facilities and procedures concluding in October. It was intended that all the airlines would transfer from Tegel by 8 November, and the first flight to land was a special EasyJet flight from Tegel on 31 October, leaving for London the next day.

The rest is history, as they say. In the next few days, Europe shut down again, banning foreign travel without exceptionally good reason. The majority of business meetings were now being done online with Zoom or Teams, so with no leisure travel, the system began to crumble. Like dominoes, airlines toppled, and with many less airlines the need for airports was much diminished. Governments had to decide which to keep open, and with the history of Brandenberg and ongoing union problems, the axe fell.

That was really very helpful. Previously there had been Class C airspace surrounding EDDB, and that had extended over both Schönhagen and Eggersdorf, so would have affected what they hoped would be the latter part of the flight. Now SkyDemon only showed the RMZ up to 1000 feet around Schönhagen.

Concern

Sure enough, the ankle was starting to hurt. But what was also concerning was how well they could now see the other Cessna. For most of the journey, they had clear skies and sunshine, and simply kept it in sight on SkyDemon. But now it was in much plainer view. It was no nearer, but as the afternoon waned and the temperature dropped, mist began to form, and the silhouette became sharper against the grey overcast beneath them.

Once past Frizlar, the other Cessna had started a gradual descent. The upper winds were giving no advantage. In fact, there was little wind of any direction. Their track took them just south of Magdeburg/Cochstedt (which again stretched up to FL100), but there was nothing else to worry about, except perhaps the weather.

The pilot was happy to fly on instruments, indeed, he enjoyed it. It had got him out of trouble on many an occasion when he had to resort to an SRA or ILS to cloud break. And around Kent there is a lot of water where a cloud-break over the sea is possible. But fog was different – if that was what the mist might become. He thought back to an earlier trip he had made to the north of England.

As he neared Durham Tees Valley (a.k.a. Tees-side Airport), the fog had started to roll in from the coast, and by the time he was on short final to 05, it had become a mantle over the land, and obscured the 23 threshold. The controller asked if he could see the runway and cleared him to land, but as he slowed his landing run, the fog rolled over the aircraft and all he could do was brake to a standstill. A "follow me" van was dispatched to find him, and he gingerly followed the flashing lights to the parking area.

Flying over mist, with higher parts of land or objects poking through might be an ethereal experience, but best enjoyed in early morning whilst conditions would improve, not in late afternoon as the temperature reduced, and they could worsen.

Up until now, his musings had been all about what they should do when they discovered the destination of the ghost, but they were rapidly being replaced by thoughts about safety. "We need to think about this, Colin".

Where now?

They were more than two hours into the flight and nearing Schönhagen, but the ghost was still at 3000 feet. Having listened to both Langen Information frequencies and heard nothing, they now switched to Schönhagen on 131.155, and whilst there were several aircraft on frequency, there was no sound from Sierra Mike.

Schönhagen is 135 feet AMSL, with an RMZ to 1000 feet AGL. "If he doesn't descend soon, he's not going there!".

An American-registered Cirrus on the ground called up requesting the latest weather. "Winds calm, visibility 1100m, sky clear, temperature 9, dewpoint 9, QNH 1023". "OK - we'll leave it for today and try again tomorrow" said the sensible American. If he had known his destination would be better for sure, he could have gone, but the high pressure was covering most of Germany and Poland, nowhere was sounding good, and the cooler evening was approaching quickly.

They had just passed overhead the field and although they were only a few miles behind, could no longer see the Cessna. But SkyDemon showed it in a rapid descent, until within seconds, the image disappeared from his phone.

Even if it were really low compared to them, it should have shown – unless they had turned off the transponder. What to do?

"I'm going to land whilst I can. We've lost it, and there's no point in staying up here whilst the weather gets worse. Better to make a precautionary landing, and if we have to wait until morning, we can tell the authorities what we know and make our way home. Bugger!".

He was already in the descent and scanning for a suitable

flat piece of grass. It needed to be clear enough of the fog to make an approach and ideally not less than 200m. Whilst he could land to a full stop in 80m, he wanted to be able to get out once the fog cleared. The area ahead actually looked better than Schönhagen had, but it would only be a matter of time before the options would run out.

Even a full instrument rating would not help if the local airports (Tegel was the nearest) were fogbound. The only other possibility was Precision Approach Radar from a US Airbase, where they could talk him down onto the runway (as he had practised at RAF Alconbury many years ago), but the nearest were miles to the south, and if he tried to go west to Ramstein, he would surely run out of fuel.

Another few minutes and they were over a large lake with a surface covered in mist. SkyDemon showed it as a bird sanctuary, restricted up to 2000 feet.

Whilst he did not want to upset the wildlife, he needed to get down and was sure fellow aviators would understand. As he passed the eastern edge of the lake, the area ahead was visible, and there was a large expanse of open ground with run-down buildings that could have once been an airport terminal.

More importantly, there were areas of concrete slabs resembling dispersal points and taxiways between them. There was nothing on Skydemon, nor on Garmin, but he could make a low pass to inspect, which he did.

Despite being somewhat overgrown, it looked in reasonable condition and with no wind, he descended gently onto the longest row of slabs – which at 3 slabs wide was much wider than his undercarriage, and amply long enough to come to a gentle stop. Where on earth could they be?

Nightfall

The light was now failing too, just as quickly as the fog was closing in, so rather than risk propellor or undercarriage taxying to who knows where, they shut down just in front of the "terminal". The immediate necessity as far as the pilot was concerned, was to pee. He pushed back his seat, swung out his legs, and as his foot touched the ground a pain like a knife ran through his right ankle. "Jesus!"

After relieving himself just outside the port wheel spat, he hobbled back into the cockpit to shut down all the portable electronics. Whilst the Garmin would keep working for hours off one battery charge, the Android phone gobbled juice when using SkyDemon and he already had had to turn on the reserve power-bank halfway through the last flight. The power-bank was phone-shape and size and sat in the footwell pocket by his side. It was wired to the phone attached to the windscreen. It held 20,000mAh, and could more than quadruple the life of the Samsung. As a reserve, he also had a smaller power-bank kept in the case the SkyEcho came in, and no doubt he would need that tomorrow. Maybe it was time to spend the money on permanently installed kit?

Meanwhile, Colin had also used the open-air facilities, and by the time he returned to the cockpit, the fog was as dense as the proverbial pea-soup. The light had gone completely, and with a buggered ankle, they were not going anywhere soon.

"It'll probably ease off by morning – it always does. I mean the ankle, and hopefully the fog!" The idea of spending the night upright in the Cessna had no real appeal, particularly as they had not eaten since breakfast.

Colin could help on that front. Whenever they flew together, Colin would take sandwiches. He was a generous type when it came to chipping in for fuel or landing fees (which was another reason he was always welcome) but he did not like paying cafeteria prices for sandwiches, so would take his own, sliced into strips so that he could hide them in his hand and eat them secretly, inside venues that didn't allow consumption of anything not purchased from them, whilst drinking tea supplied by them. There had not been time to eat them the previous day, so despite being a day old, they were very welcome.

Passenger Colin was an unimposing, gentle sort and quiet most of the time, but he would point out nearby aircraft in case the pilot had not seen them.

When they went to fly-ins and the like, he would wander off on his own, increasing his collection of photographs, and they would meet up at the required time to fly home again. Although they flew together, they had never really had company time whilst not in the air. Now, after sharing the contents of his holdall, Colin retired to the back seat of the Cessna to get his head down. It was surprisingly roomy.

No such luck for the pilot – he would be upright in his normal position. In an effort to abate some of the ankle pain, he swallowed a couple of Ibuprofen tablets, washed down with water from the aircraft-friendly collapsible bottle he'd picked up at a GASCO safety evening, and always took with him in case he needed it.

Lack of sleep the previous night, and the tension of the day had left them drained and it would not be long before slumber, but the pilot wanted one mystery solved at least, and used Google Maps to find the name of the place they had landed, before switching off to conserve power.

They were in Rangsdorf.

Rangsdorf

Just south of the city of Berlin, Rangsdorf had opened as an airfield on the eve of the Berlin Olympic Games in 1936. It soon became the site of the Bücker aircraft factory, building the Bü 131 Jungmann and Bü 133 Jungmeister for aerobatic sports and later, remote controlled bombs for the Luftwaffe.

During the early years of the war, the airfield became a full-blown commercial airport serving Berlin, and the Rangsdorfer See (a lake of 245 hectares) alongside served as its sister seaplane port. Later, the German Army took over the public airport and it became military grounds. The lake would later become a nature reserve.

On July 20th, 1944, Claus von Stauffenberg and Werner von Haefton departed from the airport, in the early hours, to fly to a meeting with Hitler at the "Wolf's Lair". The briefcase they were carrying contained a bomb with which they hoped to assassinate him. Left beneath the table when they exited the meeting after an arranged phone call, the case was moved by another participant, and when it detonated, Hitler's life was saved by a table leg - blocking the blast and shrapnel intended for him.

By then they were returning to Bendlerblock to celebrate and take part in the planned coup. Hitler still alive, and shortly after, they and another three co-conspirators were shot.

The Soviet Army took over both airport and aircraft factory in 1945 and operated there until Soviet troops withdrew from Germany in 1994. The Bücker factory had closed but the Soviets used it as a maintenance base for helicopters and used much of the field as an aircraft scrapyard. It was then abandoned and now, nearly all the scrapped aircraft have gone, but the buildings remain.

Our crew knew nothing of this. Dawn broke over the two cold and stiff occupants of the Cessna, and although the fog was still present, it was less dense and they could make out the structure of the terminal that they had seen yesterday and yes, it really did look like an airport.

Exploration

Being so far east dawn had come early, and there was an eerie stillness. Nothing could be heard except a train far in the distance. At least they were reasonably close to civilisation.

But the ideal would be to leave and reach the nearest airfield where they could refuel as soon as the visibility improved enough to allow it. It was important to see if they would be able to take off again, and first task was to assess the concrete. Despite the slabs having grass growing between them they were remarkably sound with no potholes or gravel. In fact, the runway they had used was in much better condition than that at the old RAF station St. Merryn, near Newquay, that he had flown into last year.

That had not been a good flying day, as on the way at about 1800 feet he bumped into a buzzard. For a split second both his and the buzzard's eye connected, and then the buzzard's legs hit the leading edge of the Cessna's starboard wing, before the bird disappeared from sight. Even a sparrow can do damage at 110 knots, and sure enough, there was an indentation when he checked after landing.

It was more cosmetic rather than true damage, and he was more concerned about his propellor being damaged by picking up stones, as had happened once before, when departing the Biggin Hill Airshow from a disused area.

But the slabs here were sound, and he paced the long row they had landed on and believed it to be 170 metres. With minimum fuel on board, it would be ample. At either end, and at another three positions along its length, there were further rows of slabs, also three abreast, at ninety degrees to his landing run, and projecting about 50 metres each side. Each of these terminated in an oval dispersal area, six slabs wide. The overall look of the arrangement was a little like a Papal

Cross, but with "arms" of equal length. It must have been for helicopters.

The position of the sun suggested it was almost east-west, and separately, there was yet another row of slabs of similar length, running north-south, but with only two dispersals attached. In both cases, the transition from slabs to grass was smooth, so if wind determined they should use the other row, it would not be a problem. But there was little wind anyway, the high-pressure system still in place over Germany, although moving towards Poland.

"We've only enough fuel to get to Schönberg, so that's our one option".

Whilst they waited for the sun to get to work on the slowly rising fog, it made sense to look at the terminal. It was a wide, low building with a curved control tower projecting from the middle. Windows were smashed and graffiti scrawled on the concrete. There were gaps between some of the boards adjacent and to the east of the tower, and they could get inside. Once through the boards there was more German graffiti and tags but also Cyrillic lettering around the ceiling line – it was presumably some Russian propaganda. Turning right they wandered through the areas, the first which appeared to have been a canteen, and the second, judging by the exercise symbols around the walls, a gym. Large holes were above them where parts of the roof had collapsed, and they needed to pick their way back through the debris to the tower.

The steps were concrete and safe. By the time they reached the top, which was effectively an open-air veranda, the mist was thin enough that they could see beyond the slabs they had landed on and view the grassed area that lay beyond. It had been a large, perfectly flat, airfield that now had random shrubbery growing here and there and occasional piles of rubbish. No runways, just a multi-directional landing field similar in size (and operation, no doubt) to the old RAF Swanton Morley. They could probably have landed anywhere on it the previous evening, provided they had avoided the odd shrub and debris, but in the fading light the slabbed runway had been a focal point and inviting.

Looking right towards the western end of the structure, the roof was in much better condition, and the furthest part looked intact. Back on ground level, an open doorframe allowed them access. On the walls were hand-painted murals of jet aircraft with the red Soviet star on their tails. Right at the end there was an almost opaque plastic screen suspended from the roof trusses, obscuring the last third of the building. Just behind the cloudy PVC, they could see something bulky with wheels, and once they lifted the flexible sheet to enter were more than surprised to find a small towable fuel bowser.

Behind it was a Cessna 172, white with blue and yellow accents.

Willkommen

Looking underneath the tailplane, in case there was a manufacturers plate with model number and registration, they found nothing. If there had ever been one, it had been removed.

As they rose from beneath the aircraft, a voice said, "Stand perfectly still" and despite that they turned to find themselves looking at one of the two men they had seen at Lognes, and a much, much bigger man wearing a black leather coat. He was holding an aluminium baseball bat and was swinging it from side to side, pointing alternately at each of them. "Oh shit".

Stunned into silence, they listened whilst the two conversed in German. The pilot had learnt German at school, and it was even one of his O Levels, but that was many, many years ago. He recognised just a few words, and the outstanding ones were *flugzeug*, which he knew to be aircraft, and *flugelspitze* which meant wingtip.

"Welcome to Rangsdorf" said the smaller man. "What are you doing here? And why are you looking at the aircraft? Please do not bother to lie, as Michael won't like it if you do". If this was Doctor Zahn talking, he spoke perfect English.

"We had to make a precautionary landing last evening. The fog was closing in and we were short on fuel. The only thing we could do was land, and there was a clearing in the fog here. We didn't mean to trespass".

"If only it was just trespass. Your aircraft was at Lognes. There aren't many Cessnas that have wingtips like that".

He was right. The Madras Supertips he had fitted some years ago, had been bought from Ace Demers in America and were quite distinctive, drooping down almost a foot at the end of each wing. Like the winglets fitted to more modern aircraft they assisted in many ways, even though the CAA would not allow any claim for better performance. He had only ever seen them on one other Cessna, but there had been similar on a Maule he knew well. In fact, he thought of them as "social wingtips" because whenever other pilots saw them, they came for a chat and asked about them. But this was not the sort of recognition he welcomed.

"So why have you followed me here and how?"

"There really isn't any point in bluffing. I can tell you the whole story, but Michael is making me nervous. I have a bad ankle, and there's no way we can run from you, so if he puts down the bat, I'll tell you".

Zahn nodded, and suggested, no, insisted, that they sat on a nearby packing case – no doubt to make it harder to suddenly move anywhere. Michael cradled the baseball bat in his elbow.

The pair of them told the story of how they knew Sierra Mike was not Sierra Mike and how it had filled them with curiosity. No mention was made of their suspicions about cargo, and they were not going to mention anything about association with Kent Police. They had theorised that the aircraft was a "ringer". Just like a stolen car with false numberplates. They were just pilot and passenger, intending to visit a museum, mad about everything to do with aviation, and just scraping together enough income to keep flying. If they could find out where the stolen aircraft went, maybe there could be a reward from the authorities or even the insurance company that had paid out on it. Having had to give up the chase, they had had to land and were intending to leave once it was suitable flying conditions, and only chanced on the Cessna whilst they were waiting. They hoped it sounded likely, and once it was said, they listened as the Germans spoke in their own language for some considerable time.

The smaller German seemed impressed with the manner in which they'd been followed. "You're a pretty smart pilot, aren't you? It would be a shame if your flying ended right here".

"More than a shame, it might as well be the end of me", said the pilot. Colin knew how he felt. Even before the second lockdown, he had missed flying so much that he almost became a case of depression. But they had never spoken about how much it meant to them both, apart from the occasional remark from the pilot about "mere mortals don't get to do this!" when they'd managed to find yet another interesting, difficult strip they could get into and out of.

"My flying, and most of general aviation in UK, is nearly over anyway. Since the second wave, there aren't enough licensed engineers alive, so no one can afford the inflated prices of those that are left. The CAA is in chaos following the departure from EASA, and similarly have hiked every fee – and that's if they can get round to signing anything off. With so many people now unemployed and taking benefits, we are being soaked by new taxes and soon no-one will fly for pleasure".

Colin listened incredulously. He had never heard him talk like that and had not considered his available transport ever coming to an end. But hopefully it was just a ploy, the pilot trying to gain empathy from another pilot? He remained his quiet self and continued to listen.

The pilot continued. "I've determined that I will fly what's left of my pension until it runs out. And when it's over, it's over. It won't be too long now, and I'll have to decide whether to crash and burn on purpose".

Zahn was impressed. Here was a fellow pilot with as much passion as him. He too had struggled financially, and to be able to continue he had succumbed to the advances made by Michael Klies. They had known each other at University whilst he had studied for his doctorate (not a medical doctor, but the title on his documents gave credence to his roleplay as they carried goods cross-border). Michael had always been a bit of a bully, he remembered, and with his large size rarely needed to resort to physical violence, the threat of it being enough.

But it was not a threat that had got him involved – it was the lure of more cash than he would need to continue flying whenever and wherever he wanted. Despite being only a private pilot, he would be paid for doing the thing he loved.

The market for illegal drugs had risen exponentially since COVID. All those bereaved people, all those unemployed. Anything to escape the total drudgery that existed throughout Europe, following Brexit and the worry of a potentially collapsing EU. Whilst he should be blaming the English for some of his troubles, in ways they had created opportunities and allowed him to keep flying.

Organisation

Klies, whose English was good, but not as perfect as that of Zahn, began quizzing his associate in German. Low tones and unintelligible to the pilot and Colin. After quite a discussion, Zahn spoke to them.

"We don't want to kill you" was a very, very welcome statement. "But we'd like you to come with us on a little journey". There really was not much point in arguing. The size of Klies and the bat in his hand did not suggest any better option.

Behind the building was an enormous SUV. The Mercedes GLS was black with darkened windows to match. The number plate began with the letter B, for Berlin. So hopefully they would not be going far. Sat in the back seat, they were told that the child locks were on, "so just sit back and enjoy the ride".

"Where are we going?"

"Not too far. You need to meet some colleagues of ours, whilst we decide what to do". Moments later Klies was locking the gates to the airfield behind them, and they were soon on the ring-road surrounding Berlin.

Klies had flunked out of university. His many interests had not really included academia, but he had followed his father's orders and tried. With no qualifications he somehow got involved in the scrap metal business. The most lucrative part of the business soon became cars. Not just wrecks but some very smart ones that were brought to his yard, for makeovers – new numberplates and locks to replace those broken whilst they were being stolen. He had met some serious people.

It was later that he also got involved with aeroplanes. His yard needed to be a real scrapyard too, and like his opposite number in Caterham, had discovered there was money to be made from spares gleaned from wrecked aircraft. Hulks that insurance companies would sell to him for a pittance. That had also led him to discover the airfield at Rangsdorf. The Soviets had left a massive number of airframes there, both helicopters and jets, and the metal was there for the taking.

The municipal plan for the field was to refurbish the buildings and build housing around them, but COVID decimated the need for offices, and no-one could afford new housing – and the council was unable to fund the project anyway. He made a ridiculously low offer for the area, promising to clean up the environment, and was surprised when it was accepted. His funds came from an organisation that brought him cars for makeover.

First step was to install the security fence around the whole area. Local kids and graffiti artists would not be playing there anymore. Then gradually, the mounds of abandoned fuselages and accompanying engines were removed and processed.

He was left with a large expanse of open ground and some decaying buildings. The cost of purchasing the land and fencing had easily been covered by the proceeds of the metal, but what to do with it now? The answer came from his financiers, who did not just steal cars.

Zahn had used his services to find second-hand parts for his Cessna. If he had had to buy new replacements from Cessna, his flying would have ended a long time ago. Cessna overpriced everything. No doubt it was an attempt to make the older heritage fleet unviable, so they could sell more new aircraft, but with new 172s at more than a third of a million, owners would do what they had to and if that meant using second-hand parts, sobeit.

One of the support brackets for his main landing gear had been found to be cracked, and his engineer would not sign it off without a replacement. Cessna wanted not only $6200 for the bracket but another $600 for the simple U-bolt to clamp the gear leg. And then there would be the cost of de-riveting the whole floor, and then the bracket. It was likely to be the annual that killed his aircraft.

And the Cessna price for spares was ex-USA – he would need to consider the cost of freight and duty.

Michael had them available from a demised 172. It had suffered a prop-strike when a student had bounced his landing and continued to bounce down the runway until the nose-leg gave way. A ruined propellor, a shock-loaded engine that was already on extension and damaged leg and lower cowling meant there was little value remaining and it became an insurance write-off, despite everything behind the firewall being intact.

Klies had listened to Zahn's requirements and decided to make an offer. One of his guys would de-rivet the donor Cessna and have the part removed and tested for cracks. It would be supplied free, but once the aircraft was signed off, he wanted a favour. The aircraft would be used to make a simple delivery, nothing heavy, but if successful he would fund all Zahn's flying for the foreseeable future.

It had been a no-brainer. Within a year he had done several trips, accompanied by one of Klies's associates, but became increasingly nervous each time. The last time he had returned and landed back at his home base Friedersdorf, where he was a tug pilot, the Polizei had turned up and quizzed him about why he was travelling to France so often.

He told the story of his childhood sweetheart there, but they still checked his aircraft paperwork. He had told Klies he would have to stop, but the organisation would not let him.

Rangsdorf provided the answer. His Rheims Rocket was repainted with the identity of a scrapped aircraft. It made sense to use a defunct British registration, as EASA and CAA hardly talked anymore, and even the co-operation between the police forces had suffered after Brexit. The aircraft would never go to England. The added logos reinforced the reasons for travel, and the organisation even managed to find a source of genuine transplant cases, from a sister gang in UK. He hoped he had become anonymous to the authorities.

Lunch

As they were ushered into the office, the bald man in gold-rimmed glasses was putting down his sandwich and taking a sip of coffee. Colin suddenly realised just how famished he was. "Take a seat. Coffee?" It was all very civilised, just like any business meeting. The office itself was quite luxurious, with a broad expanse of veneered desk between them and the man in the large leather chair. All the Germans were wearing suits, and Colin thought it an appropriate time to remove his Light Aircraft Association baseball cap, which had not left his head since before the initial take-off.

On the way there, Zahn and Klies had used the Mercedes hands-free to converse with their host. All in German of course, and the only word they really recognised was Rochester. They had heard the voice at the other end laugh momentarily.

"What do you suppose we should do with you?" It was another rhetorical question.

"I understand you come from Rochester, then? A very good friend of ours, the Dutchman, had an unfortunate incident there".

They both knew immediately what he was thinking about. A few years ago, a regular visitor to Rochester would arrive from Holland in a T-tail Piper Arrow IV, visit the Innovations Centre and then stay overnight in the Holiday Inn that sat at the entrance to the airport. But somehow drug-squad intelligence got wind of the purpose of his visits, and when they burst into room 223, they found him sat on the lavatory with his pants around his ankles, and promptly arrested him.

Importantly, they had just seized cocaine worth £2.2M from his accomplice who had collected it from him – and who when arrested, immediately told them where he had got it. The Dutchman got 22 years, and his customer 17 years. The Arrow was confiscated, left parked at Rochester for some years after his conviction and was finally auctioned off. Supposedly it was the National Crime Agency that had made the bust, but it was likely Interpol had known of the trafficking.

"We are just businessmen, you know. We would not want to punish you for discovering our secrets, but we will if we have to. You are obviously bright and know how to behave accordingly. You should use your intelligence to improve all our situations".

There was something coming, and it was not likely to be attractive, but might be much preferable to any alternatives.

"We have been missing out on a business opportunity recently, and strangely it's related to where you fly from. If we can come to an arrangement you will spare yourselves a lot of pain - or worse".

The man behind the desk continued speaking. His opinion was that to make deliveries into Kent would best be via a resident who would not raise suspicions by returning home. He would ensure that they were accompanied on the first trip in case they had any ideas of reneging on the arrangement, and their extra passenger would leave with the goods. Having made that first trip, they would be rewarded with an amount that would cover their maintenance, insurance costs, and probably most of their fuel for the year – some 10,000 Euros. This would be transferred equally into their respective bank accounts, so they both had skin in the game, and would be unable to plead innocence if they decided to betray. Furthermore, they would be given a contact number of a burner phone, that they could ring if they felt the desire to repeat the operation, which he hoped they would.

"It's quite addictive, you know – I mean making lots of money" said Zahn. He felt an affinity with the Englishmen. It was only a case of needs must that got him into it, and they must be feeling the same.

"You don't look horror-struck by the idea, so have a chat and I'll try to find some more sandwiches". That was the best offer they had had all day.

Commitment

It had not needed much discussion. They wanted to get home to their better halves, who would now be frantic with worry. Before they had left Lognes, the pilot had emailed his wife to say he would be a day longer, but not why, and similarly Colin, who did not have a smartphone, had texted home. Since then, caught up in the moment, they had not even thought about home – and even if they had, what could they have told them? And now, they were another day late.

Sandwiches delivered and rapidly consumed, the pilot spoke on behalf of them both. "No, we don't want to do it, but we will. Only we need to do it now if that is possible. If we aren't on our way home, our wives will be telling the airport that we are overdue, and people will be searching for us via our flight plan. If they have radar recordings it could lead them to both aircraft".

He had a point, thought the chairman. Better to take a quick punt and see if they were as clever as Zahn thought they were. Fortunately, there was always stock available for dispatch. But it was too late to do anything today, as in the same way Zahn normally did, they would need to route to Bitburg, an easy-going place to commence their overseas flight plan. No doubt they would need to refuel before going further, just as Zahn always did.

"You will have to stay another night, I'm afraid. Go back to your aircraft with Michael, and you can refuel and be ready for an early departure. There is a hotel on the banks of the lake – Seehotel Berlin Rangsdorf - less than 1500 metres from the airfield. Michael will stay with you there and bring you back to the field at first light. Herr Doktor will remain with you whilst you do your planning and mail or text your wives, so we know your intentions". Zahn nodded at this.

So it was that after returning to the airfield and filling up from the small bowser they were taken to the hotel with their holdalls and flight bag of planning equipment. Klies, who was obviously known to the receptionist, arranged for two rooms side by side. A twin for the English and one for himself. Zahn accompanied them to their room and watched as they immediately put all the electronics and power banks on charge. Tomorrow would be a long day and it all needed to keep working.

Planning

Two days without a wash had left them feeling distinctly unfresh. Colin was quick off the mark into the bathroom, leaving the pilots to do their stuff. The return trip to Bitburg was simple. Both Garmin and SkyDemon already had the route from Bitburg to Eggersdorf, so it was simply a task of pushing the reverse route option. The fact that they were starting from Rangsdorf did not matter, because both GPSs would adjust to their current position when activated. The previously hand-written PLOG would suffice to give all the relevant frequencies.

With normally prevalent westerly wind direction, it was likely that Bitburg would take just over 3 hours. That would mean perhaps 30-40 minutes remaining in the tanks, and if winds were particularly strong, it might be safer to drop into the gliding site at Koblenz to top up, but they would know in the morning when they could see the latest met forcast online.

After fuelling at Bitburg, the last leg would ideally have been a straight line of 246 nautical miles direct to Rochester, so well within reserves. But the restricted areas in Belgium would cause problems and it was simpler to route Sedan (LFSJ), and then direct.

Safety height from Sedan to Rochester was only 2100 feet for VFR traffic, but they would need to talk to Lille on the way through. There was nothing worse than Class D airspace, so transit would be approved. They would then climb for the crossing and would coast out just west of Calais and then coast in just west of Dover.

They would be over the sea for only 22 nautical miles, and high, so at any time could glide for the nearest land, either in front or behind dependant on progress. Although doglegging, the route had only increased to 263 nautical miles. Still plenty of Avgas.

The planning had been done on the pad, then saved to cloud, so that it could be pulled out again and loaded onto the phone.

"We only have two lifejackets, so our guardian won't have one. So that he doesn't feel uncomfortable about that, we won't wear ours – we can glide to land if necessary". There was a reason for saying this.

Before inputting the new route, the pilot saved the recorded log of the last flight into the SkyDemon cloud. That way, if things went horribly wrong and someone could access his account, they would see the landing at Rangsdorf, and that could lead then to Zahn's aircraft.

Once the waypoints were punched into both pieces of kit, SkyDemon produced a PLOG, but again having no printer, it was written out on hotel notepaper to be carried with them.

All the planning had been done quickly, and Zahn felt confident that the Englishman knew his craft. A refreshed Colin emerged from the bathroom, just as Michael Klies knocked at the door.

"I've brought you more sandwiches" he said. "But there is a trade. Give me your passports, bank cards and any currency you have". Once he had the passports, he photographed them with his iPhone. "I will return your cards and money in the morning. I want to make sure you get your rewards for helping us, and with your card information, it will be in your banks within 24 hours of our man reaching his customer. And we know exactly who you are", he said, returning just the passports.

The pilot had been glad they had not asked for anything else they were carrying. His Kent Police CPV (Aviation) warrant card remained firmly in his inside pocket. The only police powers it allowed were for him to demand a name and address, but he certainly did not want them seeing it.

"Now show me the messages you will send to your wives that you will be home within 24 hours, and then give me your phones and iPads. I will give them back to you in the morning".

The short email and text went off "Engine now fixed, can get home tomorrow". They hoped that might stop them worrying, even though until now neither wife was aware of any problems, just their lateness. The phones were turned off and handed over, along with the sole Android pad they had.

Zahn left first and then Klies. As he passed into the corridor, he turned. "Remember I'm next door. You have no phones, no money, no transport – and we have your aeroplane. Try to get a good sleep as we go at six o'clock".

With that the door closed and they were left pondering. What on earth were they going to do?

Whispers

Not knowing how thin the walls were, they spoke in lowered tones.

"We don't know who they are going to send with us yet. Hopefully it won't be another pilot. If it isn't we can say he has to sit in the back, so you can operate the radio and do other jobs for me".

"You'd trust me to do that, would you?" said Colin "only you don't normally!" It was true. Normally he did everything himself, that being his job. But he knew Colin was perfectly capable. No doubt some of the others he had flown with had let him help, whereas he only relied on him as an extra pair of eyes outside the cockpit, and company. Just to check, they talked about the radio and how the tuning worked and sure, he knew.

"If it is another pilot, I bet he'll want to sit up front so he can see what's going on. I don't want that, because if I can see any opportunities to alert anyone, I want to be able to take them. I haven't worked out any options yet, but they might arise".

He took his turn in the bath, in the hope that a long soak might relax him enough to get to sleep.

It did not, but after some hours thinking through the possibilities, he was tired enough to nod off. Besides, if it was not another pilot, he had a plan.

Day Three

It was 22 September, the day of the autumnal equinox in Berlin. The sun rose at 06.52, but by then they were already sat in their aircraft.

Before Klies had knocked on their door, they had dressed and then raided all the confectionary bars from the minibar just in case that was all the food they would see today. Klies kept to his word and the first thing he did was to hand back their bank cards and cash. "Don't worry about your hotel bill. The owners are friends, and we will settle up with them". Pity there had not been more chocolate bars to steal.

Having gathered their belongings, they were led out to the Mercedes GLS. Before boarding, they were joined by another man. "Please let me introduce your new companion, Karl". It was the other man they had seen with Zahn aboard Sierra Mike. Damn. He was obviously used to flying, but was he a pilot? He was carrying a headset bag. Double damn.

Handshakes were not exchanged. In fact, very few people ever used them anymore, even with people they *wanted* to meet. COVID had changed everything.

The four of them proceeded to the airfield, where the pilot began his checks of the aircraft and installation of the portable gadgetry.

"Karl, do you normally help Doktor Zahn with pre-flight checks?" It was a test, both for his English and his aviation knowledge.

"No, I wouldn't know what to look for. I'm just a regular bag-carrier." Phew.

"In that case, if you aren't a flier, I'd be grateful if you sat in the back seat so that Colin can operate the radios and help me with charts and the like".

Klies joined the conversation "That will be acceptable, but you should know that he has a weapon. Whilst he's unlikely to use it on his pilot he will be sat behind your friend. He is at risk if you try something stupid and Karl will be listening".

The fact that Karl had flown regularly was a little worrying, but with him sat in the back, the plan might just work!

Up until now, they had not had chance to check the forecast, but now they were all strapped in and with SkyDemon open, the METARs and TAFs for their route were displayed and it was all very positive.

They might have a few visibility problems over France as they went through a weak front, but nothing that could not be flown through.

The high pressure had been replaced, and as the sun rose, they could see a relatively high overcast that bode for smooth flying.

"Make sure you enjoy the money" said Klies before stepping back and away from the aircraft. Despite his being the only person around, the window was opened, and the "Clear Prop" warning made. It had been a cold night to leave the aircraft outside and the engine took a long time to warm up. Repeated attempts to achieve tick-over failed, and he resorted to leaning off the carburettor to negate some of the cooling from the fuel. Eventually it ran hot enough, and with mag checks and controls full and free they were ready.

Karl was seated behind Colin on the right side. His wheeled suitcase was in the luggage area with the lifejackets, and to his left was the pilots flight bag containing the extra power bank should it be needed. Karl had plugged his headset – it looked like a David Clark – into the sockets on the bulkhead behind him. There was no sign of a weapon but either a knife or pistol could easily be concealed in his jacket.

Backtracking the longest row of slabs, they made their way to the start of the runway. With just the two of them the nearly two hundred yards length would have been a piece of cake, but now with three and full tanks? To make sure of the shortest ground run, he selected ten degrees of flap.

It would not help his time to climb to fifty feet, but there was nothing of any height to be seen after the slabs ended.

He let the engine gain maximum revs before releasing the brakes. The headwind of 10 knots or so helped and they were airborne in about 160 metres – just before the slabs ran out. As soon as he took off the flap, the climb accelerated to more than a thousand feet per minute, and he gently turned onto his heading for Bitburg.

First Leg

There really was no need to talk on the radio for a considerable time. Overflying Schönhagen they were above the RMZ and it was not until Frizlar that they needed to speak, at more than halfway along the route. On the trip out they had avoided the Frizlar zone, but today they could get clearance through. They were not concerned about being overheard – the opposition was already on board.

But Colin was constantly being asked to tune into different stations. They listened for a few minutes, then tuned to another nearby. "Just listening for traffic" Karl was told. The pilot was also going back and forwards tuning in VORs, identifying their morse signals and spinning the indicator to find the radial. No doubt this was good practice, but Colin knew he would not normally do so much when the GPS was working perfectly well. And for sure, he had never seen the carburettor heat operated so many times and had been told previously that since the new engine and carb there had never been any icing. There had to be a reason that the pilot's hands were flickering around the panel constantly.

When the Cessna was originally built back in 1969, it only had a two-place intercom.

On the rare occasions the back seat held passengers, the only communication with them had been by shouting, and they missed out on knowing what was happening in front of them. David, who had died in the Spanish accident, had been an engineer and a friend as well as a pilot, and in 2010 had installed a four-place intercom to remedy the situation. A Sigtronics SPA400, it had a squelch knob to cut out unwanted noise, and importantly it had a little switch which could be flicked to turn off the rear seat sockets. This was normally helpful if the pilot needed to concentrate on a difficult task and his passengers insisted on talking.

Now he was testing whether he could turn off the rear headphones and not be noticed.

Hopefully, Karl was now bored with knobs being turned, dials spun and so on, and he did not seem to be watching particularly. He was mainly looking out the window and watching the Fatherland go by. When he flew with Zahn, they were usually much higher and today he had a much better view.

With no radio being used at the time, the pilot turned off the rear headset sockets for just a few moments. There was no reaction from behind and he turned it back on. Good. If he needed to quickly say something to Colin, he could turn off Karl for a few seconds, and by looking to his left at the same time, Karl would not see his lips moving.

Time passed and they were nearing Frizlar, which Colin duly tuned in. As it was Class E airspace a clearance would not be a problem, but it did go up to FL100, so a call was made. "Eggersdorf to Bitburg" was the only lie.

Then there was little need to speak again until nearing Büchel, but the activity around the panel continued. Whilst they had avoided Büchel airspace on the way out, they now got clearance to commence a gradual descent, and once clear, changed to Spangdahlem as their airspace almost surrounded Bitburg. Spangdahlem Tower did not want them anywhere near. The American controller asked them to route around as they were launching F-16s.

"Bugger". They had been flying for three hours already and the ankle was letting him know. Could not be helped, so they turned right and aimed for Meisburg, from where they could parallel the side of the rectangular CTR.

Colin switched to 118.705 for Bitburg, and they announced their impending arrival.

Homeward Bound

Once parked and awaiting the arrival of the bowser and van-driver, it was time to use SkyDemon to submit their flight plan for the crossing. As planned, they would pass through Luxembourg briefly and then France, and although probably no-one in France would want to speak to them, they would certainly want to know who was in their airspace.

The flight plan was easy to create. With the route already in SkyDemon, figures were adjusted for planned take-off time. Whilst all the usual information including equipment carried, aircraft colour etc. was saved, he did adjust the "persons on board" to read 003. SkyDemon did the rest and submitted it to all those who needed to know. Someone might be interested in that.

Karl had rarely spoken during the whole flight, except to ask for an occasional position report. He now suggested that he and Colin remain in the Cessna whilst it was refuelled but was told the refueller probably would not allow it for safety reasons.

"He might do, but isn't this an opportunity to stretch your legs and have a pee? I certainly need one. We can all go together, and he can refuel whilst we are away. Remember, we've got another two and a half hours flying yet".

Persuaded, Karl agreed, and once Colin had exited and pushed the front seat forward, attempted to leave the aircraft. Cessna rear seats are very roomy but exiting is not that quick and not at all easy if you forget to undo your seatbelt. They all managed to laugh and were left a little less tense when he finally emerged.

The nearby toilet block was visited, with Karl staying close behind them, except when he lined up alongside in the said building. There was no opportunity to talk to Colin.

By the time fuel was taken and the van-driver paid it was almost an hour. So quite sufficient for the plan to have reached everyone and it was time to go. They departed into the now lowering overcast. Safety height to Sedan Douzy was 2800 feet, so the hope was that the cloud would not lower too far.

The ritual of activity around radios continued. The VOR at Diekirch was tuned and identified and they flew straight over it. Twenty minutes after take-off they had passed over Luxembourg and were in France. Whilst the flight plan said LFSJ (Sedan Douzy) they were aiming for a point a little to the southeast before turning and overflying the field.

This would keep them just outside D29 and then D26, the danger areas that reached up to 4500 feet. They would also be above both the low-flying and the helicopter training areas, which only went up to 500 feet, before they turned.

After passing Sedan, which happily did not have any overhead aerobatics that day, the nice lady's voice on SkyDemon announced they were approaching a restricted area and sure enough, a large red circle was displayed on the Samsung phone. It had not been there when planning yesterday, but apparently Florennes had activated it – there must be Belgian F-16s flying too. The dogleg that would have just missed the corner of Belgian airspace, was widened to avoid the radius of the RAT.

The fortunate coincidence was that that meant they would not need permission to enter the Lille CTR but would fly just a little south of it. Still talking to Lille as they passed through their TMA, of course, but with little chance of a refusal to access. And they would still be above the CTR at Merville Calonne which only went up to 2000 feet.

It was all going quite well, except for that bloody ankle.

Blighty

Before they had reached Calais, they had seen the warning for the activated Danger Areas in the Channel. It only reached up to 1500 feet to allow the drone to weave backwards and forwards in its search for economic migrants in small boats. Whilst there had been a respite in winter, the calmer waters at present meant they were still trying constantly to get to the better life they imagined in England.

Homework might have told them it was not such a good prospect. GB had suffered more COVID deaths than any other European country, and with longer and more frequent lockdowns that anywhere else, industry was decimated and unemployment at record highs. But it was still rich pickings for the like of Klies, whose end customers would no doubt fund their habits with crime. Who knows, maybe some of the migrants would assist in the distribution?

The pilot had again tried the on/off switch to the rear headset jacks and had not been detected doing so. Maybe soon.

France was happy to see the back of the Cessna and acquiesced when they requested change to Lydd as they coasted out. Before tuning in to Lydd Approach, they quickly listened to the ATIS on 129.230 ensuring they had a good feel for the weather and QNH.

Contacting Lydd Approach, they informed them of their departure point and destination, current position (coasting out by Wissant) and estimate for Folkestone and were instructed to squawk 7066. Previously the VFR button had been activated so that the transponder automatically displayed 7000, but now instead of inputting 7066 as instructed, he very carefully selected 7500, then immediately turned the volume on the radio down to nil. He flicked off the rear intercom. "Colin, say nothing". And flicked it back on. The game was on.

Kelvin Carr

Lydd does not have its own radar, so any given squawk (usually 7066) is given so that anyone else with radar, would know that the aircraft was in contact with them. Now Lydd tried talking to the channel-crossing aircraft but could get no reply.

Kelvin Carr was manning the tower at Rochester. He was feeling happy yet concerned. He was happy because the rebuilding of Rochester was finally complete, and they were still in business. Some years previously, Rochester Airport had been lucky to receive the promise of a massive grant to not only refurbish the airport hangars, build new ones, a new hub and control tower, a new home for the Medway Aircraft Preservation Society, and even a hard runway.

Planning objectors put paid to the hard runway, and it was necessary to get on with the rest of the project or lose the available cash. The initial downside was that they had to give up one of the grass runways, so that a new business park could be built, but that sounded worthwhile as with no attention the current structures were decaying away – it would be a fair exchange.

Runway 34/16 duly closed. Archaeological digs, necessary as part of the planning permission, sprang up and decimated the appearance of the previously smart grassed areas used for aircraft parking and more. The resident aircraft owners had to decamp from their hangars whilst they were refurbished, and park in remote areas outside. Some of those with wood or fabric-covered aircraft, that must be hangared, removed them and gave their business to Lydd, or Headcorn or Biggin Hill.

So it was, that with a large part of the airport income stream removed, the project ground to a halt. Not exactly a halt, but between the council, the project managers, and the builders, everything seemed to take an interminable time. Add COVID and the inevitable lockdowns, and it seemed doomed. None of the remaining residents wanted it to fail, and many who had left, wanting to return, gave the airport management their full support, and wrote to MPs, Councillors, and anyone they thought might help to pressure activity.

The one good point (if you can call it that) is that nowadays aviation tends to be an old man's sport. Sure, there are always up and coming young pilots, but with the decimation of the airlines, there are less than previously as the career paths are limited. But aircraft *owners* tend to have achieved a reasonable income, or probably pension, and were not affected by COVID redundancies.

They continued with their passion, and eventually, when the roofs were repaired and the bricks were laid, looked forward to a new future at Rochester.

Kelvin had been all things at the airport. Manager, fueller, radio operator – when there was no-one else there during lockdown, he would be there to refuel any of the emergency services that needed it, whilst keeping an eye on everything else.

So now it was finally finished (and there was still a hope for hard runway, one day) he was happy they still had an airport but was concerned about one of his residents.

The Cessna had left for France three days ago. He knew the two occupants well. A capable pilot with a thoroughly nice enthusiast alongside him. As always, he had been copied on the GAR that Border Force and Customs receive. Under the new rules since Brexit, Rochester had been issued with a permit to accept overseas flights, but it was necessary to keep a close eye on things if that were to remain the case.

And there lied the problem. The GAR had said they would return yesterday from Lognes, France. They did not. He had not heard from the pilot, who would usually simply call him if there was a change to his plans, and yet today he had received a copy of a flight plan showing the aircraft coming back from somewhere in Germany.

Moreover, the plan said there were three people on board, and he had not seen a new GAR that would explain who the third person was.

With an eye on his licence, he had called Border Force to let them know, and they had not received anything either, but having already seen the flight plan, they were already planning to attend the arrival. There was plenty of time to get there due to the long flight.

Lydd & Southend

Lydd Tower had been unable to re-contact the Cessna. They knew from the estimate they had been given that Folkestone should only be a few minutes away from the aircraft, and as luck would have it, the HMCG helicopter was on station nearby.

The new coastguard facility at Lydd had been officially opened in July 2018 and was now equipped with Augusta Westland AW189s. Capable of 145 knots, they were equipped with all manner of devices including search/weather radar. When asked by Lydd Tower if they could see the Cessna, they swiftly obliged, climbing above their regular patrol area and moving 10 miles northeast where they could, and reported back that it was about to coast in and was flying normally. Knowing the destination, Lydd tried to call Rochester to inform them that an aircraft on its way to EGTO had lost radio contact.

Rochester's phone line was engaged. The controller at Southend had seen the same aircraft at the very edge of her radar limits – and it was squawking 7500 – the international code for hijack. She knew the aircraft from the registration displayed by its Mode S, and she also knew it was from Rochester.

It regularly performed Air Search practices within her radar area, and she would watch it execute a creeping line search until the target was found and it returned to base. She had even met the usual pilot on a planned visit to the Southend tower, and he had seemed quite bright.

But anyone can have finger-trouble when inputting a number, so maybe that was it. However, it made complete sense to call her friend Kelvin, and mention it.

Kelvin had taken note of what Anna said, and confirmed he was expecting the aircraft. He had only just put down the phone when it rang again. Lydd told the story of the lost contact and subsequent sighting by the coastguard helicopter, and between the two of them, they surmised that the error was probably that the pilot had meant to input 7600 as a signal that he had radio failure.

Nevertheless, in case they had already changed his frequency, he thought it sensible to try to call the aircraft, and relay landing instructions, in case the pilot could hear but was unable to transmit.

Over Water

They had coasted out, he had turned down the radio volume, and now he waited for some minutes before speaking to Lydd again. He went through the motions of calling them and could be heard doing so by both Colin and Karl, but he never actually pushed the transmit button on the yoke.

On SkyDemon he could see the helicopter. Unheard by the others, as only he had a Bluetooth headset, the nice lady said "Helicopter, same height, two miles behind". It was good that he had turned down the radio, because if he had received transmissions, they would have over-rode the SkyDemon messages.

"Lydd seem to have gone off air. I'll try again". And repeated the illusion. "Colin, it may be just them. Try tuning in Rochester – 122.255 – and we'll see if we can raise them, we should be in range soon".

For the first time, Karl took more of an interest. As Colin rotated the knobs, he asked "What if you can't get them?".

"Not a problem. They are expecting us – we'll be there shortly – and if it is my radio that's gone awry, I already know the winds at Lydd, so I can tell which runway it will be and make an approach".

"I'll signal that I want to land by flashing the landing lights, and if it isn't safe, they will fire a flare to tell me to go round".

Of course, he did not need to get any nearer to Rochester to be in range. At present height he could have broadcast 50 miles or more, if necessary, but after Colin had tuned in Rochester, he repeated the roleplay, calling Rochester, without actually transmitting. "I'm going to make blind calls. Maybe they can hear us, but we can't hear them. I'll tell them our intentions and that I will land on 20". The transmit button remained unpressed.

Kelvin, meanwhile, was blind calling them. "Delta India, if you are on frequency, you are squawking 7500. Runway 20 right-hand circuit is in use and the QFE is 1009". No reply. Repeat. No reply.

The pilot waited until 25 miles from Rochester and then said nothing, but thumbed the transmit button – three short taps, three long, and another three short taps. Two minutes later, the same again.

Kelvin thought he had heard the carrier waves, but listened again, and sure enough they were repeated. Border Force were almost there, but now Kelvin phoned the police.

Approach

"OK. What we'll do is join via the overhead, descending on the dead side, and if they haven't heard our blind transmissions, they will see us crosswind. Then I'll make a low pass, flashing the landing lights, go around and then land off the next circuit, unless we get a light signal".

"We'll roll right down to the end of the runway and park in front of the new tower in the hub building. That way we will be right next to the airport entrance and the Holiday Inn, and whilst we book in and explain about the radio failure, Karl can slip off".

Karl had been on enough flights to understand about booking in at the big C and seemed to accept the plan.

Now the pilot turned his face away and flicked off the rear sockets again "Colin, be ready. As soon as we come to a stop at the tower, unbuckle and fall out of the aircraft. If necessary, run towards the tower. Say nothing now". Sockets back on.

He was counting on a reception party, and because Colin would not move the front seat to give exit room, the length of time it would take Karl to extricate himself.

He just hoped that the weapon was a knife rather than a pistol, and that whoever was in the tower had heard and understood his S.O.S.

The two circuits would give any reception committee time to organise themselves.

As he made the first approach to 20, he pulled and pushed the knob operating the landing lights, on and off several times, and was happy there was no sign of any signals from the ground. A low go-around and it was circuit number two. On the downwind leg, his phone and SkyDemon showed him the image of a helicopter just crossing the Thames, and he hoped it would be a black and yellow Eurocopter coming from the new police pad at North Weald.

Rochester Airport Café

Prior to the airport rebuild, Rochester had always had a popular café. Unfortunately, it was at the back of the main hangar and had no view of the airfield itself. But it was good value, if a little smelly – a typical "greasy spoon" popular with pilots, airport visitors and quite regularly, the police. Air Search did their training sessions there, twice a month.

The new hub was a great improvement. The café now overlooked all the airport activity and even had a decent extractor fan system. Despite it being slightly more expensive than the previous version, it was still popular with the old clientele, and today that included four ARVOs (Armed Vehicle Response Officers). When the call came from Maidstone HQ on their Airwave radios, their late lunch was forgotten, and they exited immediately to be met and briefed by Kelvin.

Kelvin admitted he did not know what was occurring, but explained what he knew, and why he would appreciate their presence - just in case. Their BMW X5 was in the new car park behind the hub and out of site from the runway and apron. They split and deployed themselves behind each end of the hub, awaiting the arrival and wondering where it might stop.

The Cessna landed long into Runway 20 in case the ground was still soft, and taxying might be slow. Reaching the end, it turned to port and trundled across the grass towards the Tower. As they taxied, the pilot moved the handle on his door rearwards to unlock it, but not yet open the door, and Colin followed suit on the starboard door.

Once parked within yards of the tower, radios were powered down and the mixture leaned to shut down the engine. "Now!"

Their hands clashed between the seats as they unbuckled simultaneously, and headsets were removed and dropped on the coaming above the panel. Unlocked doors were opened in a flash, and as Karl reached into his pocket, they rolled out onto the grass. "Go! Go!" Despite his ankle, the pilot was first away. But both immediately stopped short, as they were confronted by an officer each. "We think he's got a gun!".

Karl was still struggling to get past the front seat and swing his legs onto the ground. By the time he managed it, the remaining two officers were training their Glock 17s at his head. He could only grimace and put his arms behind his head, as instructed. When told to lay face down on the ground, he complied and one officer patted him down, removing not a gun but the oversize lock-knife he was carrying.

Meanwhile, Kelvin was vouching for the other two, but they were still led to the rear of the tower to be quizzed, albeit not in handcuffs, as was Karl.

Café again

Debriefing took an enormous amount of time, but they were permitted to call their wives to let them know they were back at Rochester, and that they needed to clear up a few things.

Once the whole story had been related, they returned to the aircraft whilst the cargo was removed, and then taxied back and around onto the apron. John and the others in the fire-crew could put the aircraft away in the newly refurbished hangar. He had been promised his space back on his return from France!

As they walked back towards the hub, the X5 left with a new rear-seat passenger sandwiched between two burly officers, and £1.2M of cocaine in the boot.

Once the tea had been ordered, the pilot said "Colin, you never did tell me why you were late the day we went?"

Colin did not answer the question but simply said "Next time, can we just go to the museum at Duxford, please?".

Epilogue

Despite Brexit, liaison between UK and German police was immediate. GSG 9, the Federal Police Tactical Unit moved swiftly arresting Zahn and Klies, but neither they nor Karl were brave enough to point the finger at the bald man in glasses and he remains free.

The ghost Cessna was impounded, found to have no ARC, and was eventually auctioned off. A canny Scotsman who was temporarily living and working in Berlin, got wind of the sale and bought it at a knock-down price. He had it shipped to Perth and knowing its history, once restored and with a new CAA certificate of airworthiness, he mockingly re-registered it as G-DRUG.

He lived to regret this, as whenever he made an international flight, he would be subject to ramp checks and searches.

Last Word

Thank you for reading The Airborne Ghost. I hope you have enjoyed it as much as I did creating it and recalling earlier experiences. If you have any questions, or would like to contact me about any matter, please email me at airsearch2@outlook.com.

 And if you have enjoyed it, please consider leaving a two-sentence review on Amazon. Amazon reviews are what makes the world go round for writers!

Also by Martin Leusby

"Pilots Progress – the highs and lows of a single engine flyer" is a memoir of nearly forty years flying and Martin's struggle to improve both his skills and his aeroplane. From novice pilot to international competitor and even flying for the emergency services – all on a private pilot licence.

Fellow pilots, would-be pilots, and aviation enthusiasts will all appreciate the relaxed style and sense of humour – and learn just how much can be achieved with commitment, and how much enjoyment can be had from flying!

Reviews: "And (almost) all in one aeroplane! The author has enjoyed a special degree of adventure in General Aviation"- **Phillip Whiteman, Editor, Pilot Magazine**

"Spurred on by the positive reception to his first aviation thriller, "The Airborne Ghost", Martin has set about recording the trials and tribulations of progressing his PPL skills. The result is "Pilots Progress", a fun book, with a quirky array of tales - **Ed Hicks, Editor, Flyer Magazine**

Glossary

ADS-B – Automatic Dependence Surveillance system
ARC – Airworthiness Review Certificate
ATIS – Automatic Terminal Information Service
AVGAS – Aviation Fuel (piston engines)
CAA – Civil Aviation Authority
CTR – Control Zone
EASA – European Union Aviation Safety Agency
ED?? – Airfield code for Germany – last 2 letters identify
EG?? – Airfield code for UK - last 2 letters identify
FAI – Fédération Aéronautique Internationale (sporting body)
FBO – Flight Briefing Office
FLARM – Flight Alarm (surveillance system for gliders)
FL?? – Flight Level (figures x 100 gives altitude)
GAR – General Aviation Report
HMCG – Her Majesty's Coast Guard
ICAO – International Civil Aviation Organisation
ILS – Instrument Landing system
LF?? – Airfield code for France – last 2 letters identify
LTMA – London Terminal Control Area
METAR – Meteorological Aviation Report (for aerodromes)
NOTAM – Notice to Airmen
PAR – Precision Approach Radar
PAW – Pilot Aware surveillance system
PLOG – Pilot's (Flight Planning) Log
POOLEYS – Supplier of pilot equipment
QFE – Pressure setting at aerodrome surface
QNH – Pressure setting for regional area
RIB – Rigid Inflatable Boat
RMZ – Radio Mandatory Zone
RNAV – Area Navigation by Radio
SKYDEMON – Navigation Software (and more)
SQUAWK – Transmit an assigned code via transponder
SRA – Surveillance Radar Approach
TAF – Terminal Aerodrome Forecast
TAKE TWO – Airspace avoidance campaign

TCAS – Traffic Alert and Collision Avoidance system
TMA – Terminal Control Area
UL91 – Unleaded version of Avgas
VOR – VHF omnidirectional range (a navigation beacon)
VRP – Visual Reporting Point
ZULU – Coordinated Universal Time (UTC)

Printed in Great Britain
by Amazon

23253542R10046